DIARY

# of a Witch

Text: Valeria Dávila, Mónica López
Illustrations: Laura Aguerrebehere
Translation: David Warriner

CRACKBOOM!

Dear Diary,
I'm writing to tell you I'm weary.
I've been a wicked witch for too many years,
and it's making me teary.

It's really not very nice
(if you weren't already aware)
to have hairs on your chin
and crazy frizzy hair.

Having a big, bulbous nose
and a black, pointy hat,
eating soup with toads' eyeballs—
there's nothing fun about that!

I've decided these long black robes
just no longer work.
How about some high heels
and a black leather miniskirt?

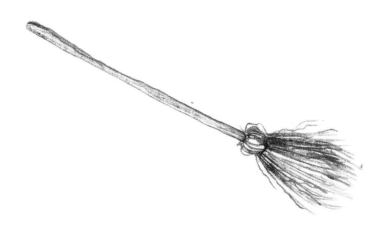

Witches straddle their broomsticks
and take flight after dark,
but I long for a nice young man
to whisk me off through the park!

But who'd fall in love
with a horrible witch
who scares kids so much
she makes their lips twitch?

I'll never find a suitor
with this stinky breath.
Surely brushing my teeth
wouldn't hasten my death?

It's a good thing, Dear Diary,
that I have my loyal cat.
He's flea-bitten and scruffy,
but I love him just like that.

CLASSIFIED ADS
ELVES
GNOMES
MUSES
ADS
RESUME
GOOD FAIRY
Very nice,
more than
meets the eye
Age: young and
sprightly
Experience : a lot
FAIRIES
COSTUMES

I'm going to get a new job
as a princess or a nice fairy
so I can wear a pink dress
and a crown that's all flowery.

Now you'll see me in fairy tales
in an enchanted castle.
Goodbye Hansel and Gretel,
and all that wretched hassle!

I must say a witch's life
is never, ever easy.
Last night a princess pricked her finger
and felt ever so queasy.

And so I cast a wicked spell
to send her to sleep forever,
but I didn't know Prince Charming
would show up and save her.

I need a real break
and am craving a trip.
And if I eat out all the time,
I'll give those beastly potions the slip!

A few days at the beach,
that's just what I need.
Time to buy a new bathing suit
with the greatest of speed!